HEALTH AND FITNESS TIPS ❀

❀ Climb stairs instead of using the elevator or escalator.

❀ Limit sweets and eat healthy snacks.

...bor's pet.

❀ Walk your pe...

❀ Help with chores around the house.

❀ Ge... ...ugh sleep ...o you're not tired during the day.

Miss Fox's Class SHAPES UP

Eileen Spinelli   Illustrated by Anne Kennedy

Albert Whitman & Company, Chicago, Illinois

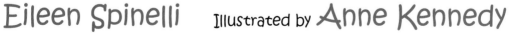

To Barbara and George Robinson.—E.S.

For Paula, always the elegant image of fitness.—A.K.

Also by Eileen Spinelli and Anne Kennedy:

Peace Week in Miss Fox's Class
Miss Fox's Class Goes Green
Miss Fox's Class Earns a Field Trip

Library of Congress Cataloging-in-Publication Data

Spinelli, Eileen.
Miss Fox's class shapes up / Eileen Spinelli ; illustrated by Anne Kennedy.
p. cm.
Summary: When Miss Fox realizes that her students do not have healthy habits, she teaches them
that healthful living is fun and rewarding, which they find to be true on Field Day.
ISBN 978-0-8075-5171-4
[1. Health—Fiction. 2. Exercise—Fiction. 3. Food habits—Fiction. 4. Schools—Fiction.
5. Animals—Fiction.] I. Kennedy, Anne, 1955- ill. II. Title.
PZ7.S7566Mj 2011 [E]—dc22 2010031471

The design is by Carol Gildar.

For more information about Albert Whitman & Company,
please visit our web site at www.albertwhitman.com.

One day when Miss Fox was reading to her class, she heard a strange noise. Frog was snoring.

Gently, Miss Fox tapped him on the shoulder.

Frog popped awake. "Sorry, Miss Fox."

The next day Miss Fox heard another odd noise.
Bunny's tummy was rumbling.
"Sorry," said Bunny. "I didn't have time for breakfast."

That afternoon at recess Miss Fox heard gasping and wheezing. It was Squirrel.

Squirrel croaked, "I ran . . . all the way . . . from the fence . . . Miss Fox."

Over the next several days, Miss Fox began to notice that many of her students had the same problems.

Falling asleep in class. (Snore!)

Not eating right. (Rumble!)

Out of shape. (Gasp! Wheeze!)

Miss Fox said to herself, "My students are not healthy."
Then she said to everyone, "This class is going to get fit!"
"So we can be ready for Field Day?" said Frog.
"Not just for Field Day," said Miss Fox. "For every day!"

Miss Fox brought the class to Nurse Weasel.
Nurse Weasel told them, "Our bodies need healthy food."
"Oh, no!" cried Mouse. "Carrots all the time?"
"What's wrong with carrots?" sniffed Bunny.
"Not to worry," said Nurse Weasel. "I have tasty recipes here for dishes with and without carrots."

After school Raccoon and her mother whipped up a batch of Mayapple Surprise.

Squirrel and his father tried the Honey Acorn Squares.

Bunny and her grandma grilled Carrot Burgers.

The following day Miss Fox asked Bunny and Raccoon to come up with some good exercise ideas for recess.

"Hula hoops!" said Bunny.

"Jump rope!" said Raccoon.

Young Bear snorted. "That's girlie stuff."

"Hold that thought," said Miss Fox.

A few minutes later Mr. Moose, the principal, was in the playground jumping rope. And Mr. Mole, the custodian, was hula-hooping.

"See, students," said Miss Fox. "There are a thousand ways to exercise."

The students got the idea—

and so did their families!

Mama Frog showed the dive that had made her a champion in high school.

The Bunny family went biking—all of them.

And the Bears whooped it up at the square dance.

A week later Bunny said, "With all the exercise I've been getting, I'm sleeping even better now."

"Not me," said Young Bear. "After watching 'Robo-Lobster' on TV, I'm too excited to sleep."

"Read a quiet story," suggested Squirrel.

"Try soft music," said Mouse.

Bear laughed. "I'm too old for a lullaby."

"No one is ever too old for a lullaby," said Miss Fox.

The weeks passed. Sometimes Raccoon wanted to play her video games. But Young Bear and Bunny made her come out to play tag.

Sometimes Mouse just wanted to eat candy.
But Squirrel shared his berries and sunflower seeds.
"It's as good as candy," said Mouse.

Sometimes when Young Bear was tempted to watch "Robo-Lobster," he would call Squirrel instead. Squirrel would sing a lullaby over the phone.

Field Day was drawing near, and Miss Fox's class was getting fit. Except for Frog. Frog continued to fall asleep at his desk.

"It's my baby sister," he told Miss Fox. "Polliwog cries real loud every night. She wakes my parents. She wakes me."

"I have an idea!" said Raccoon. She ran to the Lost and Found Box and began flipping things.

"I know I saw them . . . I know . . ."

goggles

striped toe sock

cowboy spurs

shoe

deflated soccer ball

jack-in-the-box

baseball hat

LOST + FOUND ↓

And then—"Aha!"
Raccoon handed Frog a pair of purple earmuffs.
"Try these," she said.

That night Frog put on the earmuffs. He looked
in the mirror. He had to laugh. He looked pretty silly.
Still—anything was better than not sleeping.

The following day everyone kept an eye on Frog.
Frog stayed awake all through read-aloud. And all
through geography. And spelling.
Raccoon's earmuffs had worked! The class cheered.

When Field Day finally arrived, everyone was excited.
Miss Fox's class was the Blue Team, and the Blue Team
was ready for action.

"I'm a little nervous," said Squirrel.
"Just do your best," said Miss Fox. "And don't give up."

Things did not start out well for the Blue Team.
They lost at tug-of-war.

Possum was already celebrating victory in the Lug-a-Melon
Race when she tripped over her shoelace.

But things began to go better when Frog won
the Mud Jump,

and Bunny beat everyone in the Potato Roll.

Soon the Blue Team was tied for first place. There was one event to go: the Banana Relay.

Squirrel was the last of the Blue Team's runners. Coming into the last hand-off, the Blue Team was behind. Squirrel took the banana, and with a burst of speed, he flashed across the finish line first.

The Blue Team was the winner on Field Day!

Back in the classroom, Miss Fox said, "Congratulations, Blue Team! Now I can present your fitness prizes."

"Is it carrots?" asked Mouse.

Miss Fox set a box on her desk. She had ordered buttons that read Fit=Fun. But when she opened the box she gasped. The store had given her the wrong ones!

Bunny hopped up. She gave Miss Fox a hug. "That's okay, Miss Fox. I feel peppier since I've been eating breakfast. That's prize enough for me."

"And I had enough breath to finish the relay," said Squirrel.

"And now that I'm sleeping better," said Frog, "I'm not mad at my baby sister Polliwog anymore."

"Lunchtime!" said Miss Fox. The Blue Team marched to the cafeteria to eat their healthy lunches.

Mouse came to Miss Fox. "Guess what," she said. "You've inspired me to try a carrot—someday."

"Good for you!" said Miss Fox.

Mouse put on a sad face. "Too bad I don't have one."

"I do!" piped up Bunny.

Mouse was cornered. "Me and my big mouth,"
she muttered.

She stared at the carrot. She sniffed it. "One bite—"
she said. "I'm doing this for you, Miss Fox."

Mouse took a bite. She chewed. She swallowed.
"I like it!" she shouted.
And she ate the whole thing.

HEALTH AND FITNESS TIPS

Get at least one hour of physical activity every day.

Start the day with breakfast.

Limit time spent watching TV or playing video games.

At each meal eat fruits, vegetables, and whole grains.

 Ride bikes as a family.